ALEXANDRA
THE ROCK-EATER

ALEXANDRA
THE ROCK-EATER

An Old Rumanian Tale Retold

by Dorothy Van Woerkom

Illustrated by Rosekrans Hoffman

Alfred A. Knopf New York

Text Copyright © 1978 by Dorothy Van Woerkom.
Illustrations Copyright © 1978 by Rosekrans Hoffman.

All rights reserved under International and Pan-American Copyright
Conventions. Published in the United States by Alfred A. Knopf,
Inc., New York, and simultaneously in Canada by Random House
of Canada Limited, Toronto. Distributed by Random House, Inc.,
New York.

TYPOGRAPHY BY SALLIE BALDWIN

Manufactured in the United States of America

Library of Congress Cataloging in Publication Data
Van Woerkom, Dorothy.   Alexandra the rock-eater.
SUMMARY: Alexandra cleverly outwits the dragons as she attempts
to find food for her one hundred children.
[1. Folklore—Romania. 2. Dragons—Fiction]   I. Hoffman, Rosekrans. II. Title.   PZ8.1.V452Al   [398.2] [E]   77-13778
ISBN 0-394-83536-0   ISBN 0-394-93536-5 lib. bdg.

To Sherman L. Pease
who continues to point the way
for writers in the Southwest.

D.V.W.

In the memory of my teacher,
Kady Faulkner

R. H.

Long ago, near a dark forest, lived a man named Igor and his wife Alexandra. They had a fine house, a field of turnips, and a cow that gave two pails of milk every day.

They had trees full of fruit and hives full of honey—but not a single child to call their own.

One day as they worked in their field, Alexandra pulled up a turnip and said, "How I wish we had a child to share this turnip with us!"

Igor laughed. "Only one? I wish we had *two* children to share *two* turnips." And he tossed two large turnips into their cart.

"A dozen children for a dozen turnips!" Alexandra shouted, pulling up a dozen turnips.

"*Dozens* of dozens!" Igor cried.

And they tossed dozens of dozens of turnips into the cart.

When the cart was full, they pushed it up the hill to their house. Suddenly Igor stopped. "Look!" he said to Alexandra.

Alexandra looked. There were children in the yard. Children in the trees. Children spilling out of the house and the woodshed. Dozens and dozens of children running down the hill to meet them.

"Oh, my!" Alexandra cried. "How many are there? *How many?*"

Igor was counting, "—ninety-eight, ninety-nine, one hundred. We have a hundred children," he said, smiling. "And that is not *one* too many!"

Alexandra agreed with that, and she and Igor made room in their house for every single one of them.

But their hundred children soon ate all the turnips in the field and all the honey in the hives. And they drank milk until the cow was dry.

"Before we know it, all the fruit will be gone, too," said Alexandra finally. And off she went to find more food.

he walked to the far side of the forest. It was midnight. There she saw cows and sheep on a hill, and an old shepherd tending them.

Suddenly she saw a bright green light and heard a noise like the wind. From down the road came a young dragon. He snatched a ram, a sheep, a lamb, and three fine cows from the shepherd's flock and ran up the road again.

"Come back!" the shepherd shouted. But the dragon kept on going.

"Oh, my!" said Alexandra. "That was something to see!"

The shepherd sighed and said, "Every midnight that young dragon comes and snatches a ram, a sheep, a lamb, and three fine cows."

"Well now," said Alexandra, thinking of her hun-

dred hungry children, "if I get rid of that dragon forever, what will you give me?"

"I will give you one of every three rams, one of
every three sheep, one of every three lambs, and a cow
every year for as long as you live," said the shepherd.

"Then I will do it!" Alexandra said.

She looked at the shepherd's soft round cheeses
made from the milk of his fine cows. "First I will need
one of those small cheeses and one of those large
cheeses," she said and then added, "and also a good
pocketknife."

"Help yourself," said the shepherd.

When the next midnight came, Alexandra stood in the middle of the road with the small round cheese at her feet and the large round cheese in her hand. At last she saw the green light and heard the noise like the wind.

"Stop!" she shouted.

"Dear me!" the young dragon said. "Who are you, and what are you doing in the middle of the road?"

"I am Alexandra the Rock-Eater," she said, taking a bite of the big cheese in her hand.

"And from small stones like this, I squeeze buttermilk." She picked up the small cheese and squeezed it so hard that milk came out. "If you snatch anything more from this poor shepherd's flock, I will squeeze you as small as a lizard!"

Now on the far side of a forest at midnight, two cheeses *do* look like a rock and a stone.

"Oh my!" said the dragon. "I wish I had you for a friend. Will you come home with me and meet my mother?"

"I have no time for dragons," Alexandra said. "Not with a hundred children to feed."

At first the young dragon looked sad, then he grinned. "If you will come home with me for three days, I will give you three sacks full of gold!"

"For three sacks full of gold I will come," Alexandra said. And she walked down the road with the dragon.

When they came to the dragon's cave, the mother dragon frowned fiercely and said, "Why do you bring home this weak two-legged thing instead of a ram, a sheep, a lamb, and three fine cows?"

"Listen, Momma," said the dragon. "This is Alexandra the Rock-Eater!
She is so strong that she can squeeze buttermilk out of a stone! She has
come to visit us for three days, for three sacks full of gold."

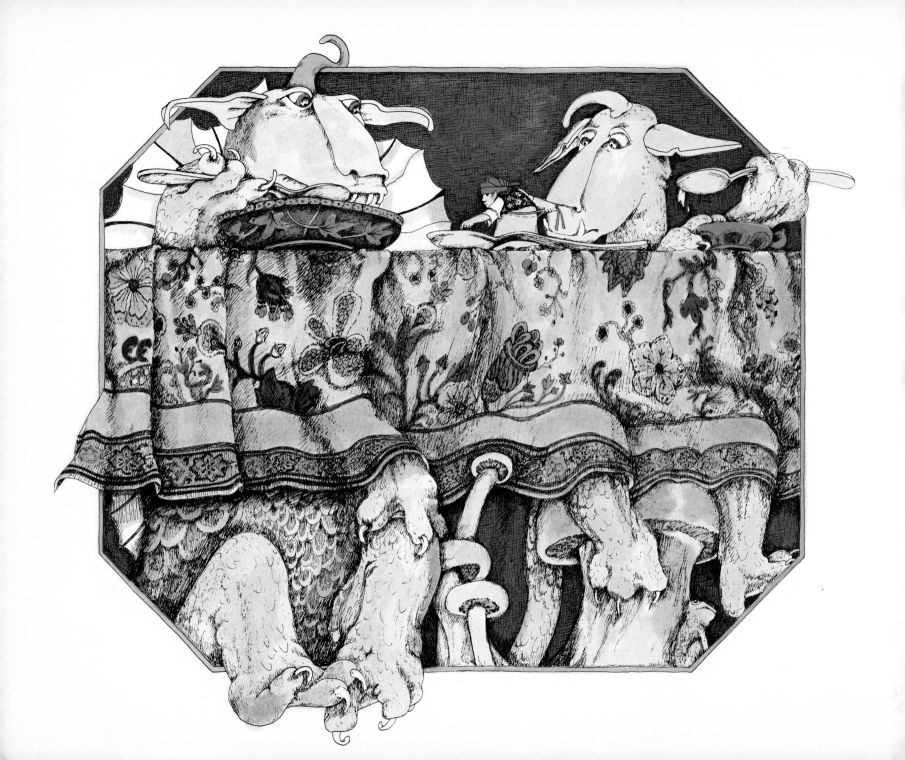

His mother snorted and rolled her red eyes. "You do find the most unusual creatures when you go out. Well, I suppose she can stay for three days," the mother dragon said with a sigh. "She is too small and puny to give us much trouble. Now sit down and eat your supper."

She poured soup into two dragon-size bowls. To Alexandra she gave a fiery glare and a dragon-size spoon full of soup.

The next day the young dragon took a club from the wall of the cave. Alexandra had never seen such a club. "Come outside with me," said the dragon. "Let's see who can throw this the farthest."

The young dragon swung the club around and around. Then he hurled it as hard as he could. It landed three miles away.

By the time they found it again, it was evening. Alexandra tried to lift the club. Not even with the help of Igor and their hundred children could she have lifted that club!

If these dragons find out how weak I really am, they will surely eat me! she thought. And then she had an idea.

"Go ahead!" cried the dragon. "What are you waiting for?"

"Can't you see?" Alexandra said. "The moon is in my way. Do you want me to hit it and put out its light?"

"Put out the moon!" yelled the dragon. "That would be terrible! We hunt by the light of the moon. I'll tell you what! Let me throw the club again, instead of you. Then the moon will be safe."

"No, I want my turn," Alexandra said. "Just wait till the moon moves a speck to the right."

But the dragon begged, "I will give you seven sacks full of gold!"

"For seven sacks full of gold, you can throw the club again," Alexandra said. And the dragon threw the club another three miles.

"Dear me!" he said to his mother that night. "Would you think that Alexandra the Rock-Eater could throw this club right onto the moon?"

His mother blew smoke through her nose. "I wish you had left that two-legged thing where you found her," she said.

The next day the young dragon said to Alexandra, "Today we must work. My Momma wants us to bring her some water." He picked up two pails and ran down to the river to fill them.

Alexandra had never seen such huge pails! She followed the dragon, watching him fill the pails and carry them home.

Now these dragons will surely find me out and eat me! she thought. Then she remembered the knife in her pocket. She knelt down and started to dig.

The dragon returned with the two empty pails.

"Now what are you doing?" he grumbled. "You had better hurry and take your turn. My Momma needs lots of water today."

"Well, that is a silly way to get it," Alexandra said. "I will just dig up the river and bring all the water to your Momma at once."

"Dig up the river!", yelled the dragon. "Then where would we go to swim? That would never do! I'll tell you what! I'll take your turn with the pails."

"Don't bother," said Alexandra, and she dug some more with her knife.

The dragon began to worry. "I'll give you seven *more* sacks full of gold," he said.

"For seven more sacks full of gold, you can take my turn with the pails," Alexandra told him.

So the young dragon carried the pails back and forth for the rest of the day.

On the third day the young dragon said, "Today we must go to the forest. My Momma needs wood for the fire."

When they came to the forest, the dragon began pulling up trees. Poor Alexandra knew that her knife would not help her now.

"Why are you standing there?" the young dragon shouted. "Pull up some trees."

Alexandra caught sight of a long vine. She began winding it around the tree trunks.

"Oh, now what?" snapped the dragon.

"It is silly to bring a few meager trees to your Momma," Alexandra said, weaving the vine around and around. "When I pull on this vine, they will *all* fall down. I will bring back the whole forest at once."

"Bring the whole forest!" the young dragon screamed. "But then where would I hide when my Momma gets angry with me? That would be the worst of all! I'll tell you what! Please let me carry the wood, and I'll give you seven times seven *more* sacks full of gold."

"All right, all right, for seven times seven more sacks full of gold, you can carry the wood," Alexandra said.

So the young dragon carried wood home till the sun went down.

That night he said to his mother, "Dear me! Alexandra the Rock-Eater is no fun *at all*. I'm glad she's going home tomorrow. Momma, she is stronger than even *Grandfather* was—and I've promised her sixty-six bags full of gold!"

"Listen to me," said his mother. "Gold is not that easy to come by. And what will we do if this creature comes back with her two-legged friends to take more from us? Tonight while she sleeps you must give her a whack on the head with your club."

But Alexandra had her ear to the wall of the cave, and she heard the plan. That night she filled a bag with sand and put it under her blanket. She said good night to the dragons, crawled under the bed, and lay very still.

The young dragon soon came tiptoeing in, with his tail tiptailing behind. He raised the club high and struck the bed with a mighty blow.

From under the bed came Alexandra's mightiest groan.

That was enough for the dragon. He yawned a wide yawn and went back to bed.

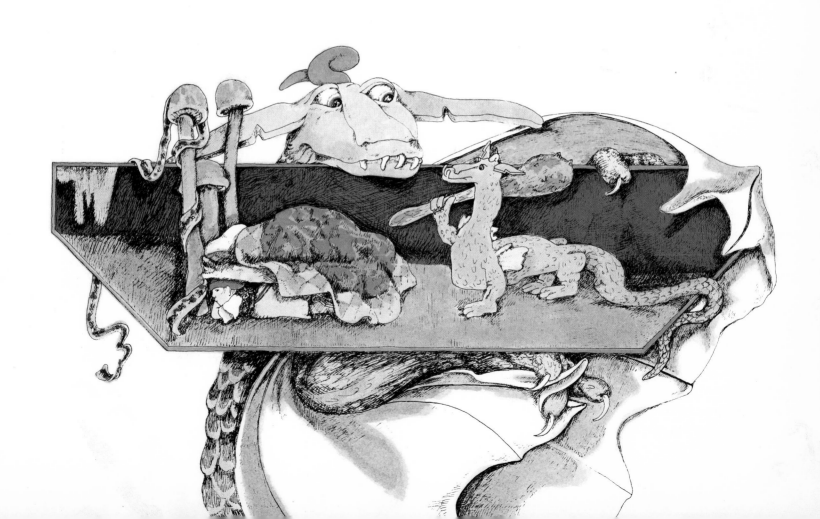

The next day at breakfast, the dragons were telling each other how clever they were when they heard Alexandra say, "Good morning."

The surprised mother dragon's spoon went clattering onto the floor. "Why, good morning," she said with a bewildered snort. "Did you sleep well?"

"Well enough," Alexandra said. "But once in the night, a pesky old flea flew into my room and bit me."

"A flea!" the young dragon shouted.

His mother jumped up and began bustling about the cave, throwing handfuls of gold into sacks. "Here," she said. "Here. And here. All this is yours if you leave right away and never return!"

But Alexandra knew she could not lift even one of those sacks.

"WHY DON'T YOU GO?" the young dragon screamed. "WHAT MORE COULD YOU POSSIBLY WANT?"

"I think I should stay for another three days," Alexandra said. "If I go home with just these few sacks full of gold, my husband will say I have no more sense than a dragon."

"Dear me!" the mother dragon shrieked. "Take seven times the number of these sacks. Or even seven times seven! Just leave!"

"Seven times seven will do," Alexandra said. "And I'll tell you what. Have your son carry these sacks, so my husband can't say that I am as weak as a dragon."

The young dragon sighed. Even the spaces between his teeth ached from his three days' hard work. But he picked up the sacks full of gold and followed Alexandra.

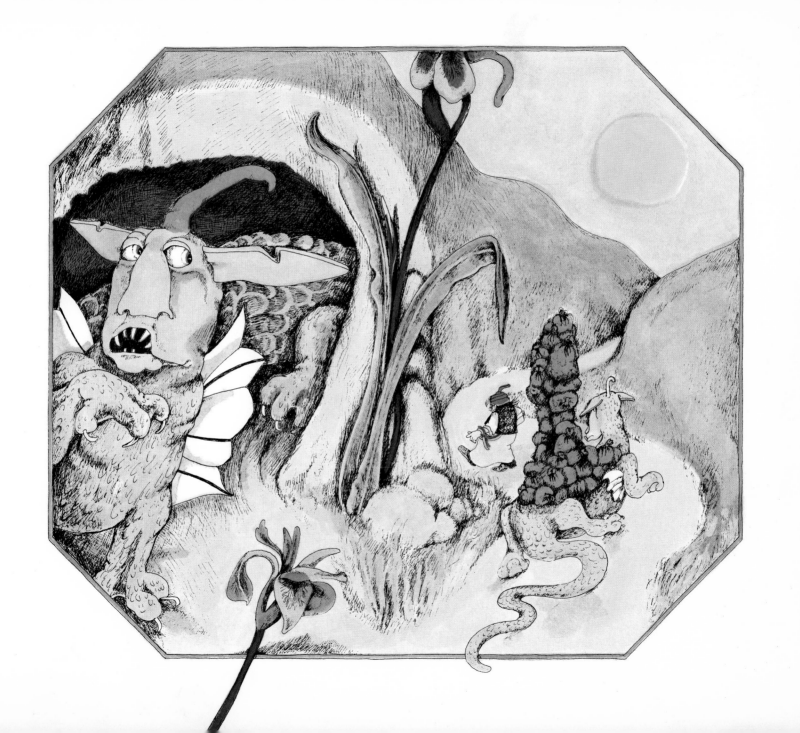

When they came to the road near her house, they saw a hundred children sitting on benches at long tables under the trees. Igor was dishing the last of the fruit into bowls.

"Oh, look!" cried one of the children. "Momma is here with a dragon! We will have dragon for supper tonight!"

Then all the children came running. The poor dragon saw, in a hundred right hands, a hundred sharp knives. He saw, in a hundred left hands, a hundred long forks. He dropped the sacks full of gold and ran.

When the shepherd on the hill saw him running away, he laughed and called out, "Goodbye, young dragon! Goodbye forever!"

"Goodbye, Alexandra the Rock-Eater!" the young dragon shouted. "Goodbye FOREVER!"

And the shepherd gave Alexandra one of every three rams, one of every three sheep, one of every three lambs, and a cow every year for as long as she lived.